FROM MY HEART

A COLLECTION
OF
POEMS

BY
JUDY STREFLING SMITH

EDITED BY
Dr. A. Thomas Smith

Bookman LLC
Publishing & Marketing

Martinsville, IN
www.bookmanmarketing.com

God's blessings to Pat
+ Sandy.

A Thomas Smith

ISBN: 1-59453-217-6

FOREWORD

These poems were written and compiled over a five year period of time by my wife, Judy Strefling Smith. Two weeks before she made her final journey to heaven to be with her Lord and Savior Jesus, God the Holy Spirit, and God the Father along with His holy angels; Judy completed her volume of poetry. Her final words to me before departing were: "The Holy Spirit told me that my work here on earth was completed and now you would have time to finish yours."

Dr. A. Thomas Smith

DEDICATION

This collection of poetry loving prepared is dedicated to the glory of God and His holy angels.

It is also dedicated to our beloved sons, Shawn Smith and Micah Smith, and to our beautiful grandchildren, Devin Smith, Autum Smith, and Seth Smith.

HAVE NO FEAR
by
Judy Strefling Smith
(January 12, 2000)

With trouble and woe everywhere that I go
I'll have no fear for my God is near!

Being buried in bills and a life full of ills
I'll have no fear for my God is near!

My marital bliss so long amiss
I'll have no fear for my God is near!

My daughter and son in trouble each one
I'll have no fear for my God is near!

With demons galore at my front door
I'll have no fear for my God is near!

Such sickness and pain and help all in vain
I'll have no fear for my God is near!
No roof for my head or a soft and warm bed
I'll have no fear for my God is near!

With death on my face where to go? To what place?
I'll have no fear for my God is near!

I WILL THINK OF HIM
by
Judy Strefling Smith
(January 13, 2000)

When my body is so racked with pain
and I feel that I will go insane
I will think of Him!

So tired of hospitals, doctors and tests
I feel that I'll never again be at rest
I will think of Him!

Feeling so scared, so frightened and alone
I just want to be free, be free to go home
I will think of Him!

When the news is not good, in fact, very bad
I feel so forsaken, so lowly and sad
I will think of Him!

Without a good friend and I'm facing my end
I feel such great grief and I look for relief
I will think of Him!

As I walk through the valley and I'm facing my death,
I know all too soon I'll be drawing last breath
I will think of Him!

I now feel such comfort, I feel His great love
I know that it comes from heaven above

I will think of Him!

As angels of wonder encircle my bed
I feel there is absolutely nothing to dread
I will think of Him!

When the moment has come and I pass from this life
I feel such gladness and freedom from strife
I will think of Him!

I have made it to heaven being given such grace
I'll live here forever with a smile on my face
I am now with Him!

THE ANGELS I LOVE

by
Judy Strefling Smith
(January 17, 2000)

In all of history whether past, present or what is to be-
His guardian angels are always there for everyone,
Yes, for you and for me!

The Lord sent His angels as guides for our life,
Caretakers extraordinaire to lead us through strife!

With unsurpassed beauty, and gowns mostly white,
They praise the Lord Jesus with great love and delight!

Their charges they treat with such warm, tender care
With dear thoughts of Heaven to lead them all there!
They battle with demons to keep us all free,
Saved to heaven our glorious Lord to see!
Great caretakers of heaven and all of mankind,
They keep all in safety and in great peace of mind!

The Lord in great wisdom, His angels of love,
Sent freely to guide us to heaven above!

TO FORGIVE
by
Judy Strefling Smith
(July 8, 2000)

I am mad, mad as I can be
How is it that the Lord
Has blessed you more than me?
Get rid of anger, bitterness, and rage
We must learn to forgive
And turn a brand new page!

My wife's a real loser,
The house she doesn't keep;
The only thing she ever does
Is watch TV and sleep.
Be careful, not to slander
Your beloved brother,
But be helpful
Love and buildup one another.
Did you hear what your neighbor
Had to say?
That your son was on drugs
And has run away.
Get rid of anger, bitterness, and rage,
We must learn to forgive
And turn a brand-new page!

How about that unwed mother
Sue Brown who lives on Taylor Street.
She doesn't care about her kids,

Not a morsel for them to eat.
Be careful not to slander
Your beloved brother,
But be helpful
Love and buildup one another!

I hate my boss; about me, he does not care.
He's mean, profane, unhappy
With nothing good to share.
Get rid of anger, bitterness, and rage,
We must learn to forgive
And turn a brand-new page!

I don't like our pastor,
His ways I just don't see.
He's so strange and unusual,
So different from me.
Be careful not to slander
Your beloved brother,
But be helpful, love
And buildup one another

There's a member of my church
We do not see eye to eye;
She gets me so angry,
So angry, I could cry
Get rid of anger, bitterness and rage,
We must learn to forgive
And turn a brand-new page!
I just heard a rumor
That could ruin your whole life,

You've been a bad husband,
Unfaithful to your wife.
Be careful not to slander
Your beloved brother,
But be helpful, love
And buildup one another

You've said I am a liar,
What I say is so untrue;
I can never be trusted,
be trusted again by you.
Get rid of anger, bitterness, and rage;
We must learn to forgive
and turn a brand-new page!

My mother doesn't care for me,
Oh, to be an only child;
She gives everything to the
Others and let's them
All run wild.
Be careful not to slander
Your beloved brother
But be helpful, love
And buildup one another

Let not the sun go down on anger
This we have been told,
Doing so will give the devil pleasure
And a very strong foothold.
Get rid of anger, bitterness, and rage;
We must learn to forgive

And turn a brand new page!

WHAT EASTER IS TO ME
by
Judy Strefling Smith
(April 15, 2000)

Bunnies of chocolate are great fun to eat-
But salvation is the real Easter treat!

Baskets of candy are lots of Easter fun-
But the most precious gift was that of God's dear Son!

Many colored eggs so vivid and so bright-
But that the Lamb rose from the dead
should be our true delight!

Beautiful spring flowers around every door-
But the real beauty is that He died
That we might live forevermore!

Easter means fresh beginnings and life anew-
And the blessed assurance the Christ died
for me and for you!

HE LOVES ME!
by
Judy Strefling Smith
(July 19, 2000)

Being born far from perfect,
A huge nose on my face;
I feel so bitter
And full of disgrace.
Upset and unhappy, I never will be,
I know the Lord, my dear God;
He really loves me!

I am so very fat,
In fact, big as a house;
I hate myself greatly,
I feel like a louse.
Upset and unhappy, I never will be,
I know the Lord, my dear God;
He really loves me!
I know I am ugly,
Oh, what can I do;
So homely, unwanted,
So depressed and so blue.
Upset and unhappy, I never will be,
I know the Lord, my dear God;
He really loves me!

My teeth are so crooked,
All over the place;
I feel so unhappy;

Not a smile for this face.
Upset and unhappy, I never will be,
I know the Lord, my dear God;
He really loves me!

They call me skinny,
I am far too thin,
I try to gain weight
But where to begin?
Upset and unhappy, I never will be,
I know the Lord, my dear God;
He really loves me!
I am wheelchair bound,
I feel such despair,
It's so very hard
To go here and go there.
Upset and unhappy, I never will be,
I know the Lord, my dear God;
He really loves me!

I know I am dumb,
I know I'm not smart,
People taunt me and tease me
And hold me apart.
Upset and unhappy, I never will be,
I know the Lord, my dear God;
He really loves me!

My life is in shambles,
I want it no more;
There is not a hope or a chance

Just closed door after door.
Upset and unhappy, I never will be,
I know the Lord, my dear God;
He really loves me!
It does not matter what color my face,
Infirmity, deformity.
I'm covered with grace;
I know my Lord loves me,
That's easy to see.
For whatever the case
He did die for me!
Upset and unhappy, I never will be,
I know the Lord, my dear God;
He really loves me!

LOVE
by
Judy Strefling Smith
(August 8, 2000)

Cling to what is good
as a real Christian should;
Hate evil and hate sin
For this is where to begin!

Be sincere in love to one another,
taking care the needs of your dear brother;
Before you go and think of you,
The needs of others do pursue!

Serve the Lord with utmost zeal,
Your loving heart to reveal,
In prayer be faithful evermore,
Your own spirit to restore!

Be joyful in hope,
Full of calm and peace;
And patience in affliction;
It should never cease!

Bless the people that do you so wrong;
Treat them with loving kindness
While singing them
A happy song!

Harmony in life

Is a very special key;
Loving one another
Is how it all should be!

For those in pain and full of sorrow;
Care for them
So that they
May see a glad tomorrow!

Proud and conceited
We never ever should be;
But peace, love and kindness
Should be our cup of tea!

Revenge is mine,
Saith the Lord,
Leave room for my wrath
And live in a forgiving accord!

If your neighbor is in need
Your goods with him do share;
Show him you love him
And for him you really care!

Always show your love,
Have a smile upon your face,
Never do evil, think first of God
And the world will be a better place!

THE PEACE OF GOD
by
Judy Strefling Smith
(August 14, 2000)

In the Lord, forever and always do rejoice;
Praising Him together in sweet and loving voice!

Show your love and kindness to everyone you meet;
To all be soft and gentle, and live at Jesus' feet.

Let nothing cause you great anxiety or fear;
Always remember that the Lord, your God is very, very
near.

In all concerns of daily living, the Lord do ask and
pray;
And give Him much thanksgiving every single day.

God wants to grant you His very special peace;
And the protection of your minds and hearts for Him
will never cease.

Whatever is noble, right and pure;
We should take special notice and ponder these for
sure.

What is praiseworthy, lovely, admirable or an excellent
sort of thing;
Think of these often, and great happiness they will
bring.

Whatever you have learned, received or heard from
Him
Or seen of Him, do pursue;
Put it into practice and the God of peace
Will be with you.

LOVE NEVER FAILS
by
Judy Strefling Smith
(August 30, 2000)

Love is forever patient,
Love is forever kind;
A special food for the soul
And a feast for all mankind.

Envious and proud it will never be;
Never boastful or rude
But friendly and kind
For everyone to see.

Caring always for others,
Putting all self needs last;
Being slow to anger,
And putting all wrongs in the past.

Love hates what is evil, no matter what the source;
It rejoices with the truth.
It hopes, trusts, protects,
And always stays the course.

Faith, hope and love;
These three things do remain;
But love is by far the greatest
And should be our life's refrain.

SPRING IS
by
Judy Strefling Smith
(April 8, 2001)

Spring rain and a warm soft breeze;
Bringing tender growth to wakening trees.

Joyous spring flowers color the land in every hue;
Sunny yellow, soft pink, luscious lavender
And bright robin's egg blue.

Farmers busily working their earthen fields,
With hopes and wishes for great and bountiful yields.

Sounds of wetland creatures croaking in the night;
Glorious birds with melodious song giving true delight.

Such a fresh, clean wind and soft scents in the air;
Rustling the bushes and blowing through my hair.

Renewed life for all God's creatures,
New births on earth abound;
It's wonderful to be alive,
Such beautiful sights and sound.

Thank you dear Lord Jesus, for all You do and give;
For the splendor of Your world on which we work and
live.

A CHRISTIAN
by
Judy Strefling Smith

"How can I become a Christian?"
Is the most important question anyone can ask;
This is no profound mystery
Or even an agonizing task.

We must realize that we
All are sinful by nature and
Yes, we all do sin;
By acknowledging this fact
Is where exactly to begin.

To be saved,
You must believe
In the Lord Jesus Christ
With all your heart;
Accept Him as your
Lord and Savior and
A grand life will begin for you,
A wonderful new start.
Confess Chirst Jesus as Lord
And believe in your heart
That God raised Him from the dead;
Invite Him to take control of your life
And you will be saved just as He said.

With Christ in your heart
Express your faith with kind actions;

Loving words and joyful sound;
Commit yourself to Him as Lord
And you will surely
Be saved and Heavenward bound.

THE RISEN CHRIST
by
Judy Strefling Smith

The tomb was empty.
His body wasn't there;
"Where had they taken Him,
Where do tell me where?"

As Mary Magdalene stood by the tomb
and cried.
Jesus spoke to her while standing at
her side.

"Don't be afraid,
There is nothing for you to dread,
Your dear Lord Jesus
Has risen from the dead!"

"Tell my disciples
To go to Galilee,
They will know I am alive
For they shall see the risen me.
On the road to Emmaus,
Two men did go;
Discussing the resurrection of Jesus,
Thinking perhaps it wasn't so.

They didn't know it was Jesus,
but with them He did walk;
The scriptures He did open up to them

In a very straight forward talk.

"Peace be with you, I am not a ghost, touch me,"
To His disciples He did say;
Their doubts and troubled minds
To forever take away.

"Go teach everyone, everywhere all about me
And baptize them in My name;
To believe in Me and be baptized
Shall save them by the very same."

Redeemed by Your suffering and death
Put us on a ground so steady;
But when you do return to judge
Will we all be ready?

He lifted up His hands, blessed them,
And departed from this earth;
To sit at the right hand of God the Father,
The purpose was completed,
The reason for His birth.

I shall spend my forever
With my dear Lord up in heaven;
I know this because
He died for me and with His grace
All sins are forgiven.

Thanks be to Jesus,
To you I give praise, and love;

All glory, laud and honor
To You in heaven up above!

GOD OPPOSES THE PROUD
by
Judy Strefling Smith

God opposes all people who are puffed up and proud;
So you don't want to be foolish and part of this crowd.

Humble yourselves, under God's almighty hand;
That He may lift you up
In the due time
That He had planned.

Give over to Him all your
Anxieties, worries and problems,
For this is the wise thing to do;
And He will take care of all of these
Because He really loves and cares for you.

Be controlled and alert every second, minute, hour;
Because your enemy, the devil,
Is like a lion
Looking for someone to devour.

The whole world suffers
Because Satan works relentlessly
To possess us all;
Resist him with all your might
And in your faith stand so very tall.

We all suffer at Satan's evil hand,
Because he does such wrong;

But the God of all grace, Himself
Will restore us making us
Firm, steadfast, and strong.

Lord, you have called to us,
In your eternal glory;
To You be all the power
For ever and ever,
For this is the best end to our story.

THE CHRISTMAS BLESSING
by
Judy Strefling Smith
(December 3, 2001)

Dear God up in heaven
We humbly pray;
To thank You for Jesus,
Your Son, born this day.
The gift of a Savior
From Your endless love;
To save us for heaven
This warm, caring dove.

A huge task to ask of
This wondrous birth;
To be Savior and King
Of all heaven and earth.
The angels, they sing
With great joy and delight,
The birth of Lord Jesus
A glorious sight!

(May be sung to the tune of *Away in a Manger*)

BEWARE
by
Judy Strefling Smith

Do Satan and his demons really exist,
Or do you say: oh, what the heck?
Believe its true, my dear friend,
Their mighty grip is on your life
And around your very neck.

They study your needs,
Every want and desire;
They tempt you and tease you
To get your soul
For hell's eternal fire.

They work with no relent
Be alert and do not tire,
They try to influence and possess
to sink you in their muck and mire.

Many darts and arrows
They do throw at you
To give you horrid dreams;
Bad thoughts to abound
In your minds, and
Oh, such awful schemes.

They whisper in all ears,
Yes, both to young and old
To do the devil's deeds;

Keep both eyes wide, wide open
To tell the flowers from the weeds.

Walk bravely through
The storms that ravage
Your dear life;
Spit on the devil's plan
For trouble and for strife.

Satan is under the feet
Of the Lord Almighty God,
So of this we must rejoice;
In loving adoration
In thankful joyous voice!

Fear not, the righteous
Do over the demons have
A just special power;
A gift of Christ, our Lord,
Our strength and watchful tower.

Just tell Satan and his demons
To leave in Jesus mighty name
And never to return;
Go to their home in hell
eternally to burn.

Say <u>NO</u> to Satan;
Repent of your sins,
The Ten Commandments keep;
The love of God the Father

And His heavenly home you'll reap.

PAIN
by
Judy Strefling Smith

Pain is my mortal enemy that just won't go away;
It grips my body and torments my mind each and every
day.

Disquieting thoughts pound in my throbbing head;
My body so frail and weak not to rise up from my bed.

All the things that I should do, but cannot really care;
Haven't the strength or desire to even comb my hair.

Family and friends give comfort - they lend a helping
hand;
But it's on my own two feet I really wish to stand.

Where can I go when only pain I know and death it
seems so right;
I wait for its approach - that sneaky thief-in-the-night.

I hope for the anguish to end, perhaps wellness perhaps
not;
But I know of true relief and peace because in my life
It's Jesus that I've got.

I do know of salvation, to believe in Christ the Lord;
I want no part of hell and of damnation,
Of Satan and his evil hoard!

Have mercy on me gracious Jesus, whether it be
recovery or my end;
I do know with certainty that you are
My best and truly good friend.

WE THANK YOU
by
Judy Strefling Smith

For the sun in the morning
For the moon and stars at night;
For all the animals of the earth
And the birds in song and flight
We thank You.

For good food and for rain
And the life that they sustain
We thank You.

For the creatures that in the waters do abound;
For a beautiful world filled with glorious sights and
sound
We thank You.

For Your angels so devine
Being such a blessing all of the time
We thank You.

For Your unsurpassed love, Your grace and
forgiving,   Your comfort and strength make a
life so well worth living
We thank You.

For the ultimate gift that of Your dear Son
Who died to save us each and everyone
We thank You.

For all that you so graciously give
We should praise and give thanks
To You dear Lord every moment that we live
We thank You.

ALL THE PRECIOUS CHILDREN
by
Judy Strefling Smith

No matter how long that we may live;
Our children to us,
Are the most precious gift
That God can ever give.

They are born needing such tender, loving care;
As parents with loving hearts for our children,
We are always, for them,
Happy to be there.

Such bright and smiling faces;
And yet feelings; oh, so, so tender;
How can one look at their child
And not all personal love surrender?

A child's love is so very perfect
And they trust always in you;
Is there any good thing in this world,
For them you wouldn't do?
Sing to them, read to them, eat with them
And of course, have fun and play;
Most importantly teach them about Jesus
And show them how to pray.

Hold them, kiss them, and teach them
Right from wrong;
All your love and attention will help them

Grow wise and very, very strong.

Tell them that you love them and for them,
You'll always care;
Baptize them in Jesus' mighty name and tell them,
For them, He will always and forever be there.

Tell them they are Jesus' little lambs
And they will always have His great love;
A love so complete and wonderful,
Sent to them from God in heaven up above.

THE TONGUE
by
Judy Strefling Smith

There should be a warning sign
Hanging on the noses of many a face;
"Danger ahead, beware,
There could be wicked tongue in place."

The tongue is a part
Of the body really rather small;
But its power is so great
That if unchecked it could ruin us all!

It can corrupt the body
From head to little toe;
Being a restless evil
And very poison foe.

To the owner, it sets their life's course
Toward eternal fire;
A pleasure and joy to Satan
To get his prime desire.
The tongue can be so very sharp
As to cut like a butcher's knife;
An evil so very formitable
To destroy many an innocent life.

With this same tongue do I praise
The Lord, my Father and honor His great name;
Then turn and curse men who in God's likeness

Is made the very same?

This sort of behavior should not exist
And be a part of me;
I must learn to tame my lethal tongue
And only love to see.

MOTHER
by
Judy Strefling Smith

M   Her love is as
high as a MOUNTAIN
She shapes young MINDS
She tries with all her MIGHT
She's worth MILLIONS to her family.

O   She's truly an
ORIGINAL
She's always doing for OTHERS
She's OUR ONE and ONLY mother
She's always OUTSTANDING.

T   She deserves
all of our THANKS
She TEACHES us the way of life
She keeps the family TOGETHER
She shows us what TRUST is all about.

H   She HOLDS
us in HER loving arms
She makes a HOUSE a HOME
She tries to HEAL our every wound
She tells us about HEAVEN.

E   Her love is
ENDURING
The love light shines from her EYES
She's an EXCELLENT friend
She's our EVERYTHING

R   She's so
RICH in love

We will always REMEMBER her
She doesn't get many REWARDS
She RAISES her children with tender loving care.

WORRY NOT!
by
Judy Strefling Smith

"Boy, am I worried,"
We too often say,
But all the worry in the world
Will not take any of the pain away.

Do not worry
About your daily life;
Doing so will only bring
You grief and strife.

What posh restaurant to frequent,
Or chic opening to attend;
Where to be seen,
But why and to what end?

When we think about tomorrow
Don't worry and don't fret;
Of worry we have not good to gain,
Only anguish do we get.
The birds that fly above us
Worry not of their supplies;
They sing sweetly of their blessings
While winging in His skies!

Worry as we might or may;
Not to our lives
Can we add

One single day!

Be of good faith,
And do not cry,
Throw your worries far away
And tell them all good-bye!

We are His own creation,
And we He truly does love;
Our needs are His concern
And will be met from heaven above.

The Lord knows our needs
For clothes, for drink and food;
He will supply all of these
And work for our own good!

The beauty of the lilies
Our clothes just can't compare;
The Lord knows all our needs
And for us He really does care!

One thing most important
Is to seek and you will find;
Your needs will be met to give you
The greatest piece of mind!

Trust in the Lord
And to Him do always pray;
Be reminded of His love
And He will keep you everyday!

HIS ANGELS
by
Judy Strefling Smith

At the moment of conception
We are sent from heaven above,
A special guardian angel
A gift of God's great love.

The Lord in His great wisdom
What kind a person I will be;
So He sends a chosen angel
That is very much like me.

Channeling and spirit guides,
Forget it and don't bother, it simply isn't so;
Be very careful and check the Scriptures,
They will tell you the way to go.

Your angel has a name and though sinless, is very much
like you.
They have likes, dislikes, interests, emotions and
feelings too.
They love the beauty of God's world,
And all that's good within;

They battle with Satan and his demons and all to do
with sin.
Abilities so exceptional to them do abound;
They move quickly from here to there
But never with a sound.

Their beauty is renowned
With gorgeous hair and face;
But their looks they can change at will,
Being any ethnicity, color, form, or race.

A great extension of our Lord with such great love and
tender care,
They work hard to protect us,
And lead us to heaven,
Our Savior to be with there.

They do not eat or drink
But do like many a special smell.
They love cleanliness and tidiness,
Things in order and in place, it does them well.

They are called to special stations,
Each one of them is not the same;
Yes, each one of them is different,
But all work in Jesus' holy name.

Your angel can hear you,
They know everything you do and say,
They are always with you,
And will never go away.

In great appreciation,
We praise You, our dear and loving Lord,
For your angelic realm
Working for heavenly accord.

CHRIST IS COMING SOON
by
Judy Strefling Smith

Overcome yourself, the world and Satan,
Repent and fervently pray;
The end of the age is coming soon,
Perhaps even this very day!

The time is here, with atomic and hydrogen bombs.
Biological and biochemcial weapons on the shelf;
Humankind can completely destroy everything
On this planet, yes, all of life and self.

There will be godlessness
As decent society will be no more;
Perilous times will come and touch
Every heart on every shore.

The horror of this is just the beginning,
As Bible prophecy will be fulfilled;
Great trials and tribulations are soon coming;
When all human blood will be chilled.
Satan relentlessly sends his arrows and probes
To each and everyone;
Seek God and His truth, zealously pray,
And believe in Jesus Christ the Son.

Do not focus your life on the love of money,
Selfish pleasures and things of no real worth;
Set your mind on things above in heaven

And not of things on this earth.

Prophesy reveals that soon, after the bloodiest battle
In the Middle East, a fifteen year war;
Christ will indeed return to judge those for eternal
punishment
or those for everlasting life and to live forever more.

The time is ripe the time is now, search out the full
truth of the Bible,
And clutch it to your heart.
With God's grace, your name will be written in the
book of heaven
From which it will stay never to depart!

IN ILLNESS
by
Judy Strefling Smith

In the name of God the Father,
And of God the Son,
And of God the Holy Spirit. Amen.

Lord, I am not well;
Almost every moment seems
As if it were spent in hell.

The pain is always there,
Sometimes less and somtimes more;
At times it's so intense of life please close the door.

Visits to doctors it seems they'll never end;
More exams and tests
How to cope and to contend?

Medications, I've had my fill,
So many pills to take;
Overwhelmed with unpaid bills,
Won't I ever catch a break?

I feel so weak and tired
So full of dread and real despair,
This body is so very sick,
Beyond all help and any repair.

I look at all that should be done

And I know that I'm not able;
No energy to do a thing
Not even set the table.

Those days and health and strength
Are gone and far away;
I know that my time is short
Seeing not many more a brand new day.

Dear Lord, draw close to me,
Let me relax in the reservoir of your peace;
Refresh me, remind me again how much you love me
And that your love, for me will never cease.

Tell me of my blessings,
Give me quite words of confidence;
Refresh me with the stability
Of you love and everlasting presence.

In the powerful and loving name of Jesus,
Lord my body please do heal;
Give me comfort, peace, and strength to endure.
For I know Your love is real.

Death, I'll have no fear,
My Savior died for me upon the cross;
Assured my sins are forgiven,
Victory over death my life will see no loss.

Let me rest in Your arms of forgiveness
And sweet eternal love; and rejoice

In the day when we shall be united,
Forever, in heaven above.

THE FIRST CHRISTMAS
by
Judy Strefling Smith

That very first Christmas
Was an oh so special day;
Because of the birth of a baby
Who had such a great role to play.

Christ Jesus,
Was this very special child;
Born to His mother Mary,
So beautiful and mild.

In Bethlehem,
This very holy place;
Chosen for the birth
Of the one born to have great grace.

In a stable, wrapped in cloths,
What a humble birth;
For the King of Kings of all the heavens
And Savior of the earth.
While shepherds watched their flocks
In fields quite nearby;
Angel Gabriel did appear to them
From the heavenly night sky.

He told them good news
Of such great joy;
That the Savior had been born,

A glorious baby boy.

And the angels praised Him
From the sky above,
"Glory to God in the highest and on earth
Peace to those that have His love."

With such great love and true compassion
To earth He did come;
To die for the salvation
Of each and everyone.

Hallelujah! We adore You
For all that You have done;
Our sweet Saviour Jesus
And God's beloved Son.

HAPPY BIRTHDAY DEAR JESUS
by
Judy Strefling Smith

I really do love Christmas
It's full of fun and joy;
I'd like to go to every store
And buy up every toy!

Party after party,
Good things to eat and drink;
My minds in such a boogle
It's hard for me to think!

Christmas tress and decorations,
Lights glowing in the night;
Do the cooking and the baking
So many cards and notes to write!

Buy the gifts and do the wrapping,
Anything else to put upon my list;
Oh, to have two more hands
To willingly assist!
All the hustle and the bustle,
Too many things to do and places where to go;
I think this gives me pleasure
Then I think maybe it's not so!

I've been to every store and mall,
But still feel empty after all;
Could it be that I've forgotten

The real reason for this joyous season?

To remember the birth of Jesus,
God's beloved Son;
Is the real meaning of Christmas
So joyously celebrate, celebrate it everyone!

Happy birthday dear Jesus,
Happy birthday to you.
Happy birthday, dear Jesus
We really love You!

DADDY DEAR
by
Judy Strefling Smith

Daddy, dear it's hard to believe
That you're not with me anymore;
Your worldly life has ended you now know peace and
glory.
You've gone through the heavenly door.

At times you were not
All I wanted you to be,
But perhaps you had trials and tribulations
You wouldn't let me see.

I hope you knew I loved you
I tried to tell you so;
But the words did not come easily
Somehow they didn't flow.

I wanted to be the best of children,
Heaven knows how hard I'd try;
Always working to gain yur approval and when
thwarted
My heart would break and it made me cry.
When I became a parent
I found it not to be an easy task;
There is so much to know and unending questions
To answer and to ask.

When my life is over

And I leave this imperfect world for that perfect
heavenly place;
Only love and true happiness I'll know
As I once again look upon your face.

GONE IS MY BELOVED
by
Judy Strefling Smith

My beloved one has died
And lives on earth no more;
Their mortal life is over,
They've completed their worldly war.

My eyes are swollen
With so many, many tears;
Where has precious time gone,
Life filled days and years.

My lonely heart is aching,
I feel a cavernous void.
Oh, to see my dear one again
To hear another word.

My body feels such emptiness,
I just can't bear the pain;
My life has no direction,
Wishing no longer to remain.
Anguish, agony and sorrow
Fill my every day;
Loneliness an enemy so very great,
How to make it go away?

All those special memories
Going through my muddled head;
How dare I keep going on

I wish I too were dead

In prayer I cry out for God's strength
To sustain me in my sorrows;
And with heart and mind attune to His presence,
I will see glad tomorrows.

Jesus Christ is my strong tower,
This to me He does always show;
The closer I become to Him
His peace to me in ways the world will never know.

I must remember that He cares for me
And abandon me He'll never,
His heart is bound to me
In love for always and forever.

LONELINESS
by
Judy Strefling Smith

I'm so lonely
Oh so totally alone;
I've got no one to adore
And to call my very own.

I eat my morning cornflakes,
No one to look at across the table;
To find a special someone
I've not been blessed or able.

Alone, it's no pleasure
As I go out to shop or dine;
I would really love someone to join me
That I might call them mine.

How I long for someone who really cares,
To have a conversation or engaging talk;
A warm hand to hold
As I take a stroll or walk.
At night, in lonely solitude
As I sleepily wander to my bed;
I wish for that special someone to share
The pillow where I lay my head.

The Lord, in His great love,
Gave to all a guardian angel our life with them to share;
So we are never really alone because

For us they're always there.

We all seek love and this I do believe;
That the Lord God is always at my side
And promises me in love
That He will never leave.

Although at times, I feel lonely
And it seems no one is there;
Jesus and His precious angels
Always keep me in their loving care.

JESUS' BIRTHDAY
by
Judy Strefling Smith

Christmas is a time of special fun;
For you, for me, for everyone.

Lots of presents you can see;
Piled high beneath the Christmas tree.

It fills our hearts with great delight;
Knowing our Savior Jesus was born this night.

SPECIAL PRAYERS
by
Judy Strefling Smith

Dearest Lord with thankful hearts
We do pray for all the blessings
For this day. Amen

As the sun rises
We begin a brand new day;
Lord, keep your arms
Around us and by our sides do stay.

I ask all that I ask in Jesus' mighty name. Amen.

Dearest Lord with thankful hearts
We do pray for all the blessings
for this day. Amen.

I worry about my children
As they travel through this life;
Lord, please guide them and protect them
So they suffer very little strife.

I ask all that I ask in Jesus's mighty name. Amen.

Dearest Lord with thankful hearts
We do pray for all the blessings
for this day. Amen.

Let me see the best in others
And for their cares to pray;
Lord, help them in their needs
And keep them on Your way.

I ask all that I ask in Jesus' mighty name. Amen.

Dearest Lord with thankful hearts
We do pray for all the blessings
For this day. Amen.

My eyes are filled with tears,
My heart is full of woe;
Lord, guide me in all my ways
And tell me how to go.

I ask all that I ask in Jesus' mighty name. Amen.

Dearest Lord with thankful hearts
We do pray for all the blessings
For this day. Amen.

Grief, it fills my heart
And grips my life;
Lord, I pray for Your comfort
To help with this strife.

I ask all that I ask in Jesus' mighty name. Amen.

Dearest Lord with thankful hearts

We do pray for all the blessings
For this day. Amen.

Fear grips my fragile life
And tears at my heart;
Lord, unfold in Your loving arms
And from me never part.

I ask all that I ask in Jesus' mighty name. Amen.

Dearest Lord with thankful hearts
We do pray for all the blessings
For this day. Amen.

Lord, I'm asking for your help
My health is poor and frail;
Please send me your sweet comfort and strength
As I go along life's trail.

I ask all that I ask in Jesus' mighty name. Amen.

THE AWAKENING
by
Judy Strefling Smith

As a Christian, I've been through
Many trials and much strife;
To save many, I will tell you of
The very worst time of my life.

My first child was a gorgeous
And sweet baby boy;
Even just to look at him
Would fill my heart with joy.

The heartbreak began when
He started his career in school;
He struggled with his work
And couldn't abide a rule.

As he grew,
The troubles, they did too;
How in the world could I
Hope to bring him through?
The days and nights were dark
As discord it did brew;
People saying, "How could this child
Really belong to you?"

The things he did and said
Would hurt me to the bone;
How could he do such things,

Oh, that he would be no more;
Such peace to be alone.

Seeking help for him
Came never to an end;
Anyone out there to solve
And be a friend?

My life was hell,
I'd look at him with scorn;
Things so bad, to curse
The day that he was born.

Mental illness,
The experts they would say;
How about some more pills
To take the hell away?

In word and deed
His life a real hell;
Worldly help and jails
Did not to do him well.

After many years,
An angel in a dream did let me know;
That a demon was in charge
Of my son's hellish show.

The demons hungerly prowl,
Even the innocent to possess and hold;
They work hard to ruin

This being in their hellish mold.

To fool us as to their existance
Lets them do their job too well;
But we must know that they are many
And of their tricks from hell.

Do not think that their deeds
Are things of ancient past;
They are here and now
Until the day is last.

We must fight Satan with a faith
In God that is righteous and so true;
To tell Satan and his demons
To leave in Jesus' mighty name
Is the victory thing to do!

LET'S MAKE A DEAL
by
Judy Strefling Smith

It's hard to hear and so frightening too;
But Satan's demons are closely watching you.
Your desires and wants they listen all too well,
With lies and full intentions to lead you straight to hell.

They love to taunt and tease with now, "Let's make a deal."
Their generous promises are sure to make you reel.
Anything is possible, just name it, they will surely let you know.
Use caution and beware, for it's hell's door they will slyly show.

The demons quietly watch trying to influence and possess;
But with God's help you can beat them with great power and success.
Stand forever strong in faith and firmly let them know;
That you want no part of them and back to hell they go.

Nothing can compare to Jesus, no, nothing can compare;
The greatest desire should be Him,
and a place in heaven to with Him share.

SATAN IS NO FAIRY TALE
by
Judy Strefling Smith

Satan and his demons are no myth and certainly no
joke;
They prowl the Earth viciously humans to prod and to
poke.
For us to do their bidding gives them happiness and
pride;
Their goal leading us to hell and to their evil side.

They use all the tricks in the book, anything to make us
their very own;
They want to take us away from God and from His
mighty throne.
They can walk among us guised in beautious human
form
and even as a friend;
But, with caution and great faith do walk for in hell
They do wish us to end.

They also come as ghosts and ghouls, ugly creatures of
the night;
They love to spook and frighten us with their awful
sight.
They can appear as animals, inanimate objects, space
creatures,
The dead, even as angels of light, they are masters of
disguise;
We must pray to God for help, for wise and discerning

67

hearts
And not to trust our very eyes.

The terrible happenings and worst people in this world
Have a direct connection to Satan and his hell;
To realize this and fight his powers
Would for all to do so well.

To seek our Savior, Jesus,
To give Him our trust and true belief;
Will give us peace and comfort
And from all trouble bless'd relief.

ANOTHER YEAR, ANOTHER BLESSING
by
Judy Strefling Smith

Another year has come and gone
And another birthday is here;
Sometimes they are greeted with a little sadness
But should be met with cheer!

Just think of all the blessings
That the years have brought;
So many ways God has shown His love
And we've not given them much thought.

Thank you, Jesus, for another year
And all the blessings from your great love;
Blessings so generously given
From Your throne in Heaven above.

Dearest Lord with thankful hearts
We do pray for all the blessings
For this day. Amen.

Lord, my life's a mess.
I don't know what to do.
Please help me as I
Bring all my cares to you.

I ask all that I ask in Jesus' mighty name. Amen.

Dearest Lord with thankful hearts

We do pray for all the blessings
For this day. Amen.

Lord, we know this food and drink
Is a gift from you,
In good health let it
Sustain us all the long day through.

I ask all that I ask in Jesus's mighty name. Amen.

Dearest Lord with thankful hearts
We do pray for all the blessings
For this day. Amen.

Lord, calm the storms
That plague my days;
Never forget me,
Be with me forever and for always.

I ask all that I ask in Jesus' mighty name. Amen.

HIS ANGELS
by
Judy Strefling Smith
(December 18, 2002)

Anyone who knows the story of the birth of Jesus knows what an extensive and important part His angels played in this most important event.

Many of us have experienced events in our lives that we could call divine, with special help being given to us just at the right time.

I'm sure many, many, times we are unknowingly helped by His angels. The extent of their involvement here on earth could ber termed awesome to say the least.

Christmas reminds us of angels, but their presence is always with us.

Tidings of great joy!

THE GODLY HOUSEHOLD
by
Judy Strefling Smith
(March 21, 2003)

Wives, show your husband respect, honor, and
devotion;
This also will please the Lord and set sincere love in
motion.

Husbands, treat your wife with great love, as an equal
partner in life;
Do not submit her to your harshness and temper or to
loveless marital strife.

Children show your parents love, honor and respect,
Obey them in everything you do;
You will certainly please the Lord God
And He'll give a long life on earth to you.

Parents, love your children, show them how to love
By your Godly example;
Do not discourage, build them up,
Give them a slice of heaven to sample.

Invite Jesus Christ into your home
As an ever present guest;
In love always follow His ways
And you're surely to be blessed!

GOD'S RULES FOR LIVING
by
Judy Strefling Smith
(March 20, 2003)

Set your hearts and minds on things above in heaven
And not on things on this earth;
For treasures of the earth will crumble and decay,
Only that of heaven is and has the real worth.

Put to death your earthly nature;
Sexual immorality, impurity, greed, evil desires and
lust;
Rid yourself of anger, rage, malice, slander
And to remove filthy language from your lips is a must!

Clothe yourself with compassion, kindness, humility,
Gentleness, truth and love; have great patience,
Forgive as the Lord forgives you
From His mightly throne in heaven above.

Let the word of the Lord dwell in you richly,
Seek God's great knowledge and wisdom by which to
live;
Fill your heart and mind with God's all encomposing
love
Not just to have and to hold but so willing to give.

Sing His psalms, hymns of praise, the mighty spiritual
song;
Sing with gratitude and love in your heart

To our dear Lord Jesus
All the day long.

Whatever you do, whether it be in word or in deed,
Do all in the name of Jesus our Lord;
Giving thanks to God the Father,
All to Him in a splendid accord!

Judy Strefling Smith

THE LOVE OF A FATHER
by
Judy Strefling Smith
(June 3, 2003)

The best gift of a father to his child is to be;
The greatest role model for their very eyes to ever see!

His ways should be soft, gentle and mild;
Filled with unconditional love for his precious child.

He should always encourage and build-up with true
understanding and love;
Seeking guidance and strength from his Father in
heaven above.

In this world filled with so much trouble and fright;
He should be to his child, their shining star and their
guiding light.

MY MOTHER
by
Judy Strefling Smith
(April 29, 2003)

Whether I called her Mom, Mama, or Mother;
Her love for me was like none other.

She walked in kindness all the while;
Hiding her problems with a smile.

She helped me find faith and hope and love;
And sent many prayers to God above.

She held me closely as a child;
To calm my fears with her heart so mild.

My warm, loving Mother with a lovely face;
A true blessing to me that no one can ere replace.

BIRTHDAY BLESSINGS
by
Judy Strefling Smith

God truly blessed your parents
On the great day of your birth;
For they brought forth a special child,
A great addition to this earth.

May your days be filled with happiness
And may your blessings overflow;
May you know true faith,
Hope and love everywhere you go.

HAPPY BIRTHDAY DEAR JESUS
by
Judy Strefling Smith
December 4, 2000

I really do love Christmas
It's full of fun and joy;
I'd like to go to every
store and buy up every toy!

Party after party,
Good things to eat and drink;
My mind's in such a boogle
It's hard for me to think!

Christmas trees and decorating
Lights glowing in the night,
Do the cooking and the baking,
So many cards and notes to write!

Buy the gifts and do the wrapping,
Anything also to put upon my list?
Oh to have two more hands
To willingly assist!

All the hustle and the bustle,
Too many things to do and places where to go,
I think this gives me pleasure
Then I think maybe it's not so!

I've been to every store and mall,

But still feel empty after all;
Could it be that I've forgotten
The real reason for this joyous season?

To remember the birth of Jesus,
God's beloved Son;
Is the real meaning of Christmas.
So joyously celebrate, celebrate it everyone!

Happy birthday dear Jesus,
Happy birthday to you.
Happy birthday dear Jesus,
We really love you!

THE FIRST CHRISTMAS
by
Judy Strefling Smith
December 4, 2000

That very first Christmas
Was an oh so special day;
Because of the birth of a baby
Who had such a great role to play.

Christ Jesus, was this very special child,
Born to His mother, Mary,
So beautiful and mild.

In Bethlehem, this very holy place,
Chosen for the birth
Of the one born to have great grace.

In a stable, wrapped in cloths
What a humble birth,
For the King of Kings
Of all the heavens
And Savior of the earth.

Entering our world as flesh,
He left behind His heavenly glory,
What a wonderful beginning
To this real Christmas story.

While shepherds watched
Their flocks in fields quite nearby;

Angel Gabriel did appear to them
From the heavenly night sky.

He told them good news
Of such great joy;
That the Savior had been born,
A glorious baby boy.

And the angels praised Him
from the sky above,
Glory to God in the highest
And on earth peace
To those that have His love!

With such great love and true compassion
To earth He did come;
To die for the salvation
Of each and everyone.

Hallelujah! We adore You
For all that You have done;
Our sweet Savior Jesus
And God's beloved Son.

*(Written about the Baroda, Michigan,
cross in the Ruggles Cemetery.)*

LOOK UP!
by
Judy Strefling Smith

Look up everyone and see
The wondrous cross made of a tree,
Made from a heavenly lightning strike
For all to witness and to see.

People on a pilgrimage come to see this miracle,
They come from near, from far and wide;
To experience this act of God and feel
His presence in the quiet countryside.

A sign from God, you can bet
And believe that it is true
He certainly loves and cares for all
And this should comfort you.

He beacons you to come close to Him,
Especially in times like these;
Look up to God for help and blessings
As you pray to Him upon your knees!

LOOK UP, MY DEAR FRIENDS, LOOK UP!

The Godly Physician
by
Judy Strefling Smith

It is a noble calling to be chosen as a physician by the
Lord;
To work with the Master Physician in a wonderful
accord!

To care for His lambs with a soft and loving touch;
With infinite knowledge and a desire
For healing that means so very much.

To be in a quest to help each person
No matter their condition or their station;
Remembering all are God's children
And His love covers all, from nation unto nation.

Seeking always for mankind that higher ground
For healing and freedom from illness and from pain;
In self, being vigilently humble, meek and mild,
Not always looking for fame, personal wealth and gain.

Thinking with a sharp mind and a loving,
compassionate heart;
Makes the difference from ordinary
To one who is dynamic,
God pleasing and so very, very smart

Keeping the Lord Jesus in your life
And following His example now and for forever;

Praying fervent prayers for all of those that touch your
life;
And for all that you endeavor.

March 19, 2003

The Godly Teacher
by
Judy Strefling Smith

One of the most important professions in this world
Is that of a child's teacher;
To be the greatest teacher in the world
You must live and learn to be a reacher!

To be a recher you must apply your heart
To everything you teach,
Being loving and kind to every child;
Patient and understanding, slow to anger
With a temperment so mild.

Always there to nurture,
Praise and build up are such integral parts;
A warm smiling face together
With that guiding hand
Will reach those tender little hearts.

Showing your life as a shining example,
Being generous and so willing to love and to share;
Will teach them how to treat each other
Showing them to care.

For you to pursue what is right
And to always do what is good;
Making it your forte to do good deeds;
Will teach the young ones to be
beautiful flowers and not fields filled with weeds.

Teach them with Jesus' gentleness,
With a Godly heart and a faith in Him so strong;
For them your prayers forever and abundant,
To help keep them on the right path
And never to go wrong.

JESUS OF NAZARETH
BY
JUDY STREFLING SMITH

To Gethsemane He went to pray with grief, distress and
sorrow.
He knew that He must die for all man's sin on the not
too distant morrow.

No justice for this sinless man as the crowds cried,
"Crucify!"
But instead, Barabas, the murderer, was released the
throng to satisfy.

The soldiers put on the King a purple robe and crown of
prickly thorn.
The punishment was so severe, such mockery and
scorn.

They hung Him on a cross in a place called Calvary-
Our sins were laid upon His head, His death for you and
me.

And Christ prayed, "Father, forgive them; for they
know not what they've done.
Such love and such compassion His heart fairer than the
sun.

Darkness came over all the land, the sun was bloted out.
"My God, why have you forsaken me?" Jesus queried
with anguished shout.

Jesus cried aloud and breathed His very last.
The curtain of the temple torn in two as His precious
life had passed.

His body placed into a tomb cut out of solid rock-
They rolled a stone against the tomb the entrance for to
block.

Three faithful women came to the tomb early on the
third day.
On approach, they were heard to ask, "but who will roll
the stone away?"
The stone was moved, the body wasn't there-
But in the tomb were two angels, so beautiful and fair.
"He is not here." we've come to say
For the great Lord, Jesus, has risen today!

Glory in the highest risen is the Lamb.
A mighty price He has paid for our salvation!
How very glad I am!

CONTACT THE EDITOR

Dr. A. Thomas Smith
15344 S. Lakeside Road
Lakeside, Michigan 49116

269 469 1262
atsmith@triton.net